ARCADE WORLD

DINO TROUBLE

WRITTEN BY **NATE BITT**
ILLUSTRATED BY **JOÃO ZOD**
AT GLASS HOUSE GRAPHICS

LITTLE SIMON
NEW YORK   LONDON   TORONTO   SYDNEY   NEW DELHI

LITTLE SIMON

AN IMPRINT OF SIMON & SCHUSTER CHILDREN'S PUBLISHING DIVISION • 1230 AVENUE OF THE AMERICAS, NEW YORK, NEW YORK 10020 • FIRST LITTLE SIMON EDITION JANUARY 2022 • COPYRIGHT © 2022 BY SIMON & SCHUSTER, INC. ALL RIGHTS RESERVED, INCLUDING THE RIGHT OF REPRODUCTION IN WHOLE OR IN PART IN ANY FORM. LITTLE SIMON IS A REGISTERED TRADEMARK OF SIMON & SCHUSTER, INC., AND ASSOCIATED COLOPHON IS A TRADEMARK OF SIMON & SCHUSTER, INC. • FOR INFORMATION ABOUT SPECIAL DISCOUNTS FOR BULK PURCHASES, PLEASE CONTACT SIMON & SCHUSTER SPECIAL SALES AT 1-866-506-1949 OR BUSINESS@SIMONANDSCHUSTER.COM. • THE SIMON & SCHUSTER SPEAKERS BUREAU CAN BRING AUTHORS TO YOUR LIVE EVENT. FOR MORE INFORMATION OR TO BOOK AN EVENT CONTACT THE SIMON & SCHUSTER SPEAKERS BUREAU AT 1-866-248-3049 OR VISIT OUR WEBSITE AT WWW.SIMONSPEAKERS.COM. DESIGNED BY NICHOLAS SCIACCA. ART SERVICES BY GLASS HOUSE GRAPHICS • ART BY: JOÃO ZOD, MARCELO SALAZA & WATS • COLORS BY: MARCOS PELANDRA & KAMUI • LETTERING BY: MARCOS INOUE. THE ILLUSTRATIONS FOR THIS BOOK WERE RENDERED DIGITALLY.
THE TEXT OF THIS BOOK WAS SET IN CC SAMARITAN.
MANUFACTURED IN CHINA 1121 SCP
10 9 8 7 6 5 4 3 2 1
LIBRARY OF CONGRESS CATALOGING-IN-PUBLICATION DATA
NAMES: BITT, NATE, AUTHOR. | GLASS HOUSE GRAPHICS, ILLUSTRATOR.
TITLE: DINO TROUBLE / NATE BITT, GLASS HOUSE GRAPHICS.
DESCRIPTION: LITTLE SIMON PAPERBACK EDITION. | NEW YORK : LITTLE SIMON, [2021] | SERIES: ARCADE WORLD ; 1 | AUDIENCE: AGES 5-9 | AUDIENCE: GRADES 2-3 | SUMMARY: TRAVIS AND JOURNEY ARE BEST FRIENDS WHO LOVE GOING TO ARCADE WORLD, A MYSTERIOUS ARCADE FILLED WITH VIDEO GAMES NO ONE HAS EVER HEARD OF, SO WHEN THEY LEARN THE DANGER OF THE GAMES COMING TO LIFE, THEY MUST SAVE THE WORLD FROM PIXELATED MINIBOSSES. IDENTIFIERS: LCCN 2021017771 (PRINT) | LCCN 2021017772 (EBOOK) | ISBN 9781665904643 (PAPERBACK) | ISBN 9781665904650 (HARDCOVER) | ISBN 9781665904667 (EBOOK). SUBJECTS: LCSH: GRAPHIC NOVELS. | CYAC: GRAPHIC NOVELS. | VIDEO GAMES–FICTION. CLASSIFICATION: LCC PZ7.7.B536 DI 2021 (PRINT) | LCC PZ7.7.B536 (EBOOK) | DDC 741.5/973--DC23
LC RECORD AVAILABLE AT HTTPS://LCCN.LOC.GOV/2021017771
LC EBOOK RECORD AVAILABLE AT HTTPS://LCCN.LOC.GOV/2021017772

CONTENTS

LITTLE SIMON 2022

YOU KNOW, NOW MIGHT BE A GOOD TIME TO TELL YOU HOW WE GOT HERE.

CHAPTER 2

IT STARTED AT ARCADE WORLD.

ARCADE WORLD

ACTUALLY, WAIT. IT DIDN'T START THERE.

IT STARTED WITH AN EMPTY BUILDING.

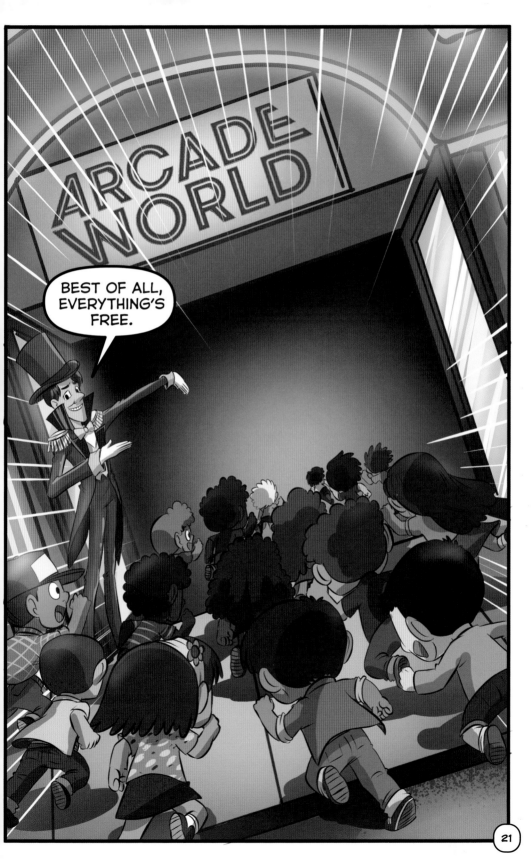

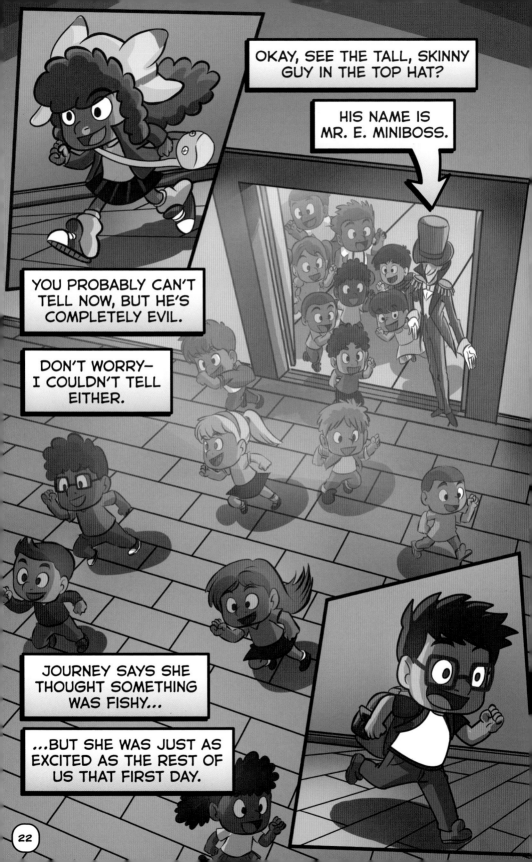

IT WAS HARD TO SEE CLEARLY WHEN YOU CAME FACE-TO-FACE WITH...

IT HAD A FEW GAMES WE'D PLAYED BEFORE.

BUT WE'D NEVER SEEN MOST OF THE GAMES.

IT WAS A WHOLE NEW WORLD.

BUT THE VIDEO GAMES AT ARCADE WORLD WERE TOTALLY NEW!

LIKE ZOMBIE INVADERS!

ROBOT BATTLE!

EARTH TO ALIENS!

DRAGON FLAMES!

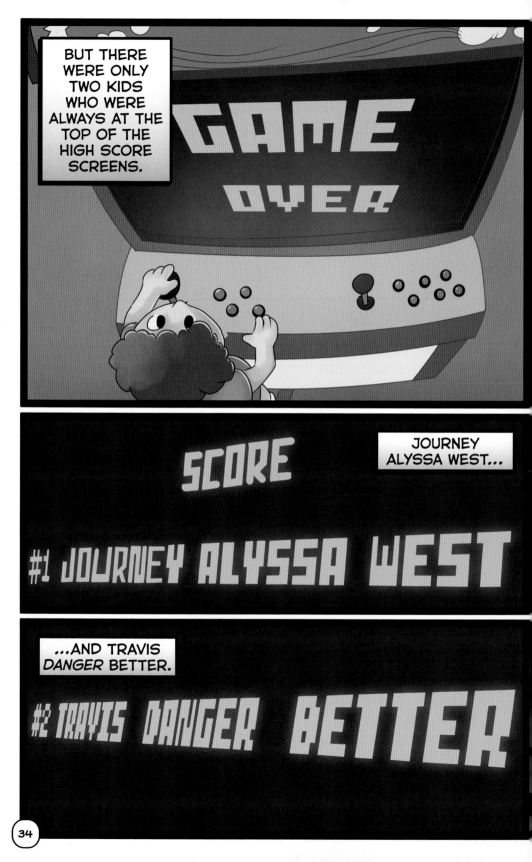

BUT THERE WERE ONLY TWO KIDS WHO WERE ALWAYS AT THE TOP OF THE HIGH SCORE SCREENS.

GAME OVER

JOURNEY ALYSSA WEST...

SCORE

#1 JOURNEY ALYSSA WEST

...AND TRAVIS DANGER BETTER.

#2 TRAVIS DANGER BETTER

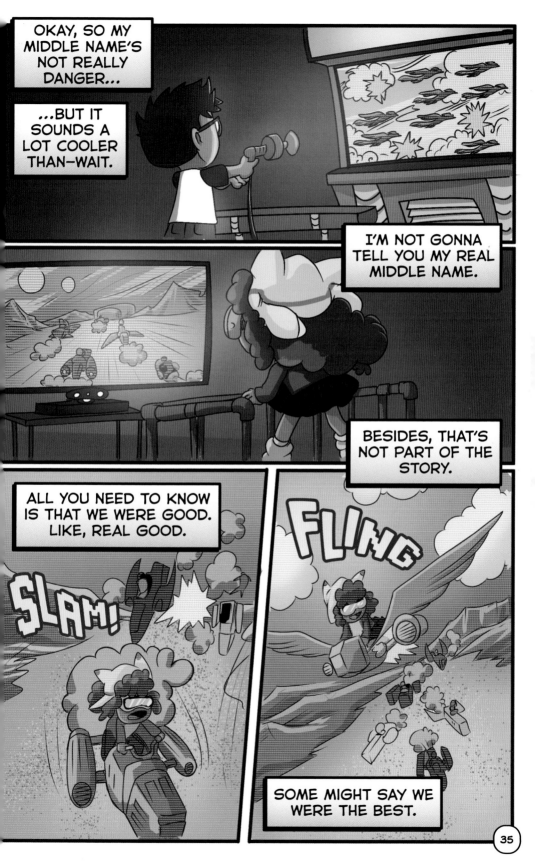

BUT BEING THE BEST
WAS WHAT GOT US
INTO THIS MESS.

NOW IT WAS TIME TO DEFEAT THE BIG BOSS: SPARKLE SAURUS.

MY DINO SQUAD WAS READY AND WAITING.

THE GLITTER DACTYLS FLEW ME TO THE SPARKLE SAURUS'S PALACE.

THE ICE CREAM IGUANODONS LED ME THROUGH THE CASTLE GUARDS.

SPLAT!

FINALLY THE SUGAR RAPTORS GIFTED ME THEIR CANDY KEY TO OPEN THE SUPERSWEET PORTAL.

ONCE UNLOCKED, I'D BE IN THE LAIR OF THE SPARKLE SAURUS.

CREAK

I COULD EVEN BEAT JOURNEY'S TOP SCORE.

NOTHING COULD STOP ME NOW. I COULD FEEL IT. VICTORY WAS MINE!

IT WAS LIKE A DRAGON AND A BIRTHDAY CAKE HAD AN ADORABLE BABY...

...AND THEN TRAINED THAT BABY TO SCORCH EVERYTHING IN SIGHT!

CHAPTER 4

YUCK. I HATE POLLEN.

YEAH, THIS STUFF GETS EVERYWHERE.

AT LEAST MY ALLERGIES AREN'T ACTING UP.

NORMALLY I'D BE A SNEEZE MACHINE WITH THIS MUCH POLLEN IN THE AIR.

YOU DON'T NEED TO REMIND ME.

I STILL REMEMBER YOUR EPIC "SNOT ME" SNEEZE.

IT'S NOT ME.

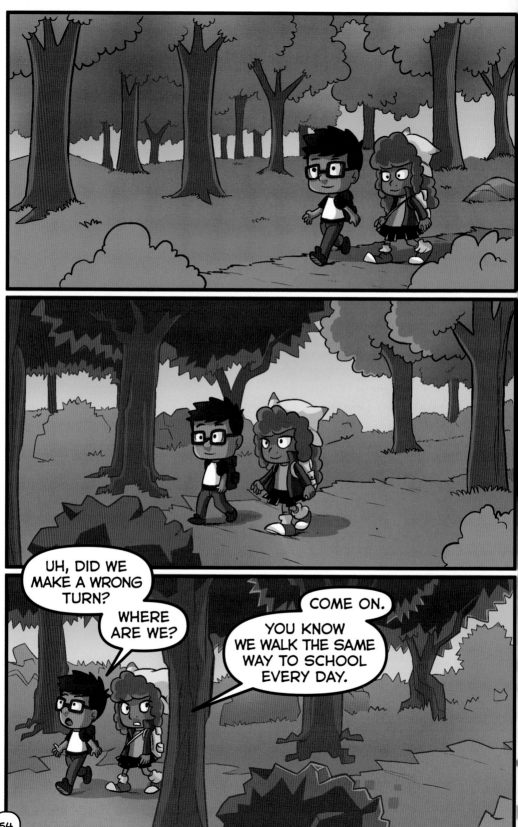

CHAPTER 7

ICE CREAM IGUANODONS!

THAT'S WHY WE RUN!

ICE CREAM CONES! WE NEED TO FIND ICE CREAM CONES. THAT'S THE ONLY THING THAT CAN HANDLE THE FREEZE.

ROAR!

RIGHT.

LET'S JUST STOP BY TWO SCOOP AND EXPLAIN WHAT'S GOING ON.

I'M SURE THEY'LL BE COOL ABOUT IT!

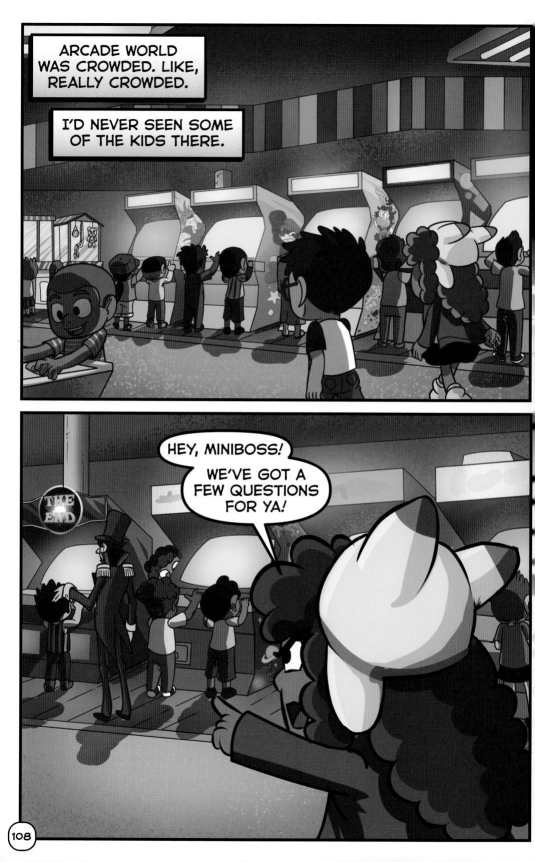

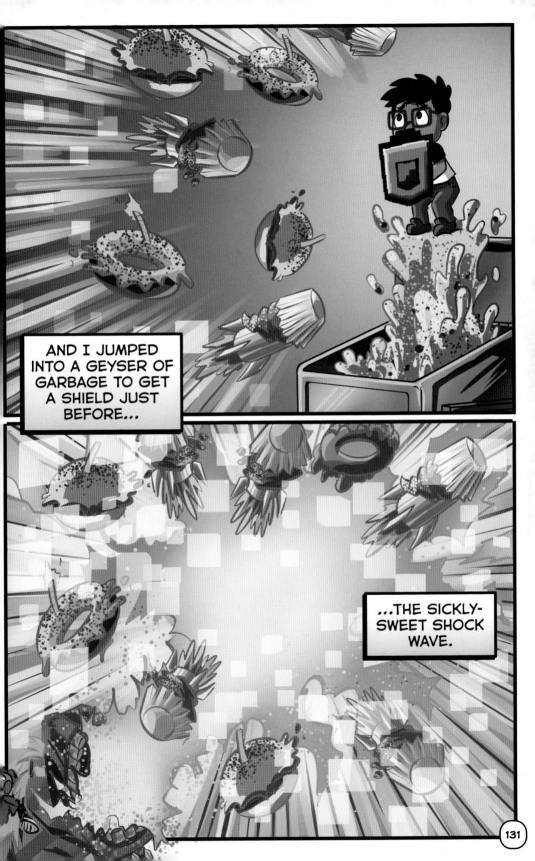

AND I JUMPED INTO A GEYSER OF GARBAGE TO GET A SHIELD JUST BEFORE...

...THE SICKLY-SWEET SHOCK WAVE.

CAN'T GET ENOUGH OF THE **ARCADE WORLD**? CHECK OUT THE NEXT ADVENTURE...

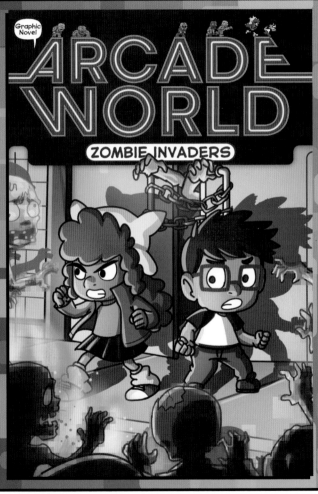

TURN THE PAGE FOR A SNEAK PEEK...